AUSSIE BITES

Bernice Knows Best

Hugh was a walking-talking
disaster without any friends
until he met Bernice.
Her specialty was in curing
accident-prone boys. But Hugh
was a challenge even for Bernice.

which Aussie Bites have you read?

 BERNICE KNOWS BEST
Max Dann
Illustrated by Stephen Axelsen

 TEACHER'S PEST
Max Dann
Illustrated by Stephen Axelsen

 NO PLACE FOR GRUBBS
Max Dann
Illustrated by Peter Viska

 MOVING HOUSE
James Moloney
Illustrated by Tom Jellett

 GOLDFEVER
Justin D'Ath
Illustrated by Rachel Tonkin

 MISS WOLF AND THE PORKERS
Bill Condon
Illustrated by Caroline Magerl

Aussie Bites

Bernice Knows Best

Max Dann

Illustrated by Stephen Axelsen

Puffin Books

For mum and Wal.

Puffin Books
Penguin Books Australia Ltd
487 Maroondah Highway, PO Box 257
Ringwood, Victoria 3134, Australia
Penguin Books Ltd
Harmondsworth, Middlesex, England
Penguin Putnam Inc.
375 Hudson Street, New York, New York 10014, USA
Penguin Books Canada Limited
10 Alcorn Avenue, Toronto, Ontario, Canada, M4V 3B2
Penguin Books (N.Z.) Ltd
Cnr Rosedale and Airborne Roads, Albany, Auckland, New Zealand
Penguin Books (South Africa) (Pty) Ltd
24 Sturdee Avenue, Rosebank, Johannesburg 2196, South Africa
Penguin Books India (P) Ltd
11, Community Centre, Panchsheel Park, New Delhi 110 017, India

First published by Oxford University Press, 1983
This edition published by Penguin Books Australia, 2001

1 3 5 7 9 10 8 6 4 2

Designed by Melissa Fraser, Penguin Design Studio
Series designed by Ruth Grüner
Series editor: Kay Ronai
Typeset in New Century School Book by Post Pre-press Group,
Brisbane, Queensland
Printed and bound in Australia by McPherson's Printing Group,
Maryborough, Victoria

National Library of Australia
Cataloguing-in-Publication data:
Dann, Max, 1955– .
Bernice knows best.
ISBN 0 14 131123 1.
I. Axelsen, Stephen. II. Title. (Series: Aussie bites).
A823.3

www.puffin.com.au

One

Everything started to go wrong the minute Hugh was born.

He poked Doctor Haroomphum in the nose by accident.

The big old doctor sneezed, and the nurse stepped back out of the way and bumped the trolley. It rolled across the room, and hit Doctor Fahfahfah in the knee. She jumped and honked like a car horn and landed on one of Doctor Krumdumdum-numnum's toes. Doctor Haroomphum lost his balance, fell backwards and made a big hole in the wall.

Then they had a door straight through to the waiting-room.

Nobody knew it was just the beginning.

People came and stood around
Hugh's cot and went *ooh* and *ah* and
pulled faces. They laughed at him
falling over his rugs and dropping his
Teddy into the bath.

'Who's a clumsy boy then?'

It was Hugh.

And when he leaned out of his pram outside Fifi Foot's shoe repair shop and accidentally pulled the brake off, nobody really gave it a second thought.

Hugh sped down the hill, ran over Mrs Rawling's groceries, made a big long scratch across the vicar's new car, squashed the vicar's lemon-meringue pie, went through some red traffic lights and ended up in Ms Willow's extremely rare and precious fine-china display.

'It was just one of those things,' they said.

TWO

Hugh's Great Aunty Agatha came to stay. She even brought her cat. She bustled and sighed a lot and her legs made rubbing noises when she walked.

SQUEAK
SQUEAK

She made a great fuss over Hugh at
first. She took him for walks, turned
herself into an aeroplane, and read
him stories about princes and elves.
She was a lot of fun.

She even stayed on after he stood
on her cat's tail by accident.

The cat jumped up and landed on
the dog, the dog leapt onto the roof
and slid back down and collided with

Hugh's dad (who was busy doing
something with the TV aerial). They
both crashed through the laundry
ceiling and splashed into the bath.

Aunt Agatha was already in the
bath.

But who could blame Hugh for that? He'd only just learnt to walk.

Then Hugh opened the oven door and her big dress caught on fire, and he broke her special bowl trying to put the fire out.

She left.

'He's not just accident-prone,' she huffed, 'he's a menace.'

They never saw Aunt Agatha again.

Three

The years passed but things only got worse for Hugh. All of those people who'd called him cute, and sweet, didn't come around any more.

Hugh's name was muttered in hushed
tones around the neighbourhood.

Old friends crossed the street
if they saw him coming their way.
The houses on either side of his
became vacant.

His tortoise ran away to Grace's
house where it would be safe. His dog
was hiding in the backyard
somewhere and hadn't been seen for
two years, and the cat disappeared
altogether.

Only his brothers and sisters and mum and dad stayed. They had nowhere else to go. They wore helmets and protective body armour at the dinner table.

By the time Hugh had turned eight,
his house had caught fire twelve times,
the plumbing had stopped working,
the garage door had jammed and
wouldn't open again, the bath had

sprung a leak, all the chairs had collapsed, and his dad's roses hadn't flowered for three years.

'Why me? Why me? Why me?' Hugh asked.

But nobody answered him.

Then something happened.

Four

He met Bernice.

She wasn't scared. She didn't need helmets, or protective armour, or any of that stuff.

'You wouldn't like me,' said Hugh,
'I'm accident-prone.'

'Who says?'

'Everybody.'

She shook his hand then and said,
'Well, you're in luck, Pugh.'

'It's Hugh.'

'Because accident-prone is my business.'

She decided then to make it her business.

Bernice was clever too. She could think of a new cure for Hugh to try out every day. And sometimes, if she

really thought about it, she could think of two at once.

There was the Left Right Off On Inside Out Cure.

'Okay, Pugh.'

'It's Hugh.'

'Now, first you have to stand on your head, undo your shoe-laces without bending your legs, and count to fifty. Got that? Then put your left shoe in your top pocket, hang your right shoe from your nose, and take your cardigan off and put it back on again inside out forty-five times.'

It didn't work.

Then there was the Frog Cure.

'This one's real easy,' Bernice

promised him. 'All you have to do is

carry the frog around in your pocket

for two days. Except for when you eat.

Then you have to bring it out and hold it in your hand.'

It was the biggest frog Hugh had ever seen. It was bright green and slippery, and did the breast-stroke to itself all the time.

Hugh put on his baggiest trousers and wore gloves. He hated frogs.

Next came the Hot and Sweaty Cure.

'You have to put on all your clothes,' Bernice instructed him. 'And then perform a double back-flip triple-twist from a handstand.'

It took Hugh nearly all day to get dressed.

Five pairs of underpants, three pairs of shorts, six pairs of long pants, eighteen singlets, nine shirts, two jumpers, twenty-seven socks, nine pairs of shoes, one pair of mittens, three hats, and one duffle-coat.

He didn't know how to do a double
back-flip triple-twist from a
handstand. He didn't even know how
he was going to stand up once he had
everything on.

Bernice even made him a cake.

'This'll fix you up for sure. It's a recipe I got from the hidden south-west corner of the Kilimanjaro,' Bernice told him.

Hugh had to spend a week in bed after eating that cake.

Five

Then one day he gave up.

He'd tried everything. Swinging
round and round on the clothes-line,

hanging onto a peg by his teeth, walking backwards and forwards to school every day with his shoe-laces tied together, sleeping in a bed full of nuts and bolts, and swimming the whole length of the Footscray Baths with a bowling ball in each hand.

Nothing had worked.

'It's no good. I'll always be an oaf.'

He wasn't going to try any more of Bernice's cures, and it was just as well. Because she couldn't think of any more.

Hugh became even gloomier than before. Not even Bernice was going to fix him, and she was so smart that

she even read the newspapers
sometimes.

'A drive in the country, that's what
he needs to cheer him up,' his mum
said.

'Yes, some fresh air,' his dad agreed.

Hugh didn't like drives.

He said, 'If you take me, I'll only break something.'

'Buck up, Hugh,' Bernice said. And to make sure he did, she went along too, and sang every single Patagonian folk song she knew.

Six

They drove and drove for hours, until they finally stopped somewhere high up in the mountains.

While Hugh's mum and dad went in search of rare and unusual oyster forks in the antique shops, he and Bernice discovered a crowd of people.

'It's a bicycle race,' she said.

Hugh couldn't see. He stood up on his tiptoes and knocked the hat off the lady in front of him. When she bent over to pick it up, the pointy end of her umbrella poked the man behind, who leapt to one side with a fright and shoved Hugh and Bernice right up to the front. They could see everything then.

There was a whole row of shiny bikes lined up. And lots of

healthy-looking people with shorts on,
and muscles in their legs as big as St
Bernards'.

'Here, hold this,' somebody said.

Hugh looked up. One of the
muscliest of the lot was talking to
him. He had a moustache, and arms

as thin as wire coat-hangers.

Bernice had seen his photo

somewhere. He was one of the best.

'Here, hold this,' he said again,

'I have to pull my socks up.'

Hugh couldn't believe it. The man

was trusting him, asking him to hold

onto the bike. Nobody had asked him to hold onto anything for six and a half years.

Hugh went and stood really close to the bike, and held on so tightly his hands started to change colour.

The other riders began to shuffle about and climb aboard their bikes. The race was about to begin.

'I'll have my bike back now.'

Hugh went to move. But he couldn't. His trousers were caught in the chain.

He bent over, the cyclist and his moustache bent over, Bernice bent over. They were all bending over, pulling and poking, pushing and perspiring. His trousers weren't going to budge.

'Hold the race!' One-of-the-Best said, but nobody heard him. The starter blew his whistle, somebody else waved a flag – and they were off, whizzing down the mountainside.

Everybody except for One-of-the-Best, that is.

Hugh knew he had to do something. He rolled forward, put both his feet on the pedals and pressed down as hard as he could.

It was working. His trousers were halfway round the big cog.

'Here – I'll give you a push,' Bernice
said.

'Noooooo!'

But it was too late, she'd already
done it.

His trousers came free, the bike bolted ahead, and Hugh was off down the mountain too.

'The brakes! Put on the brakes!' yelled One-of-the-Best.

Hugh tried, and they broke.

'That's not good,' One-of-the-Best said. 'If his brakes are broken, he's got a problem. It's downhill all the way.'

Seven

Down the mountain went Hugh. Left
around the first bend, right around

the next, and left again. He was going so fast it felt like his hair was coming out.

This was the worst thing that had ever happened to him. Even worse than eating Bernice's cake.

It was so bad he didn't even notice that he was passing all the other riders.

He did the zigzag turns sitting on the handlebars, the horseshoe bend with one foot in the water bottle, the devil's elbow doing a handstand on the crossbar, and went through the water-trap with the seat stuck in his mouth.

The other riders talked amongst themselves.

'*Quel homme!* What a rider, *monsieur!*'

'A bonny lad of a rider, for sure!'

'*Si si!*'

They had come from all over the world for this race.

'*Wunderbar!* Never have I seen such an excellent rider!'

'Help! I can't stop!' Hugh cried out.

But the other riders all laughed.

'What a card!'

'*Si si!* What a joker!'

Hugh was going faster now.

He tried turning his shirt into

a parachute, dragging his feet along
the ground, pushing things into the
spokes, and even grabbing onto the
front wheel with his hanky. Still he
couldn't slow down, and he lost his

hanky, just to make matters worse.

Then he saw something.

Far off at the bottom of the

mountain was a crowd of people,

jumping up and down and waving.

'The finish line', Hugh thought, 'maybe they can help me.'

He pedalled faster so he could get there sooner.

Eight

But between him and the bottom was one lone rider. He was the trickiest, meanest, nastiest rider of them all.

It was Rotten Frank.

And if there was one thing Frank hated, it was losing. He wouldn't stand for it. He could see that Hugh was going to pass him, unless he did something in a hurry.

He stopped his bike and got off.

'Think you can beat Frank, do you?'

Nobody beat Frank in his race. He won it every year. This was Frank's race.

And just in case somebody thought they might try and beat him, he had a backpack full of Rotten things.

He tried all of them on Hugh.

Frank tried the Box Full Of Tacks
On The Road Plan, the Oil Slick
Scheme, and the Big Cigar That Made
A Lot Of Smoke Trick.

But none of them worked.

Then he tried his real special
Rotten thing. The Inflatable Tiger
That Blew Up As Big As A Train.

Too bad about the puncture, Frank.

Hugh had almost caught up.

Rotten Frank climbed back aboard
his bike and did figure eights in front
of him, but Hugh was already doing
figure nines.

Rotten Frank made loud, scary
noises, but Hugh was making louder
ones. Rotten Frank even made faces,
but Hugh flew past him like a gust
of wind.

The little crowd was yelling and

screaming. Hugh sped across the
finish line. He'd won the race!

But he still hadn't stopped.

There was a cake display dead
ahead. The Country Women's
Association had been baking those

cakes for weeks. He was heading straight for them – going to hit . . .

. . . But he missed them.

Then he was heading for the judge's stand, but he missed that too.

He missed everything. He missed Mrs Parker's Poodles, a man selling balloons, the truck that belonged to the man selling balloons, and Mrs Parker herself.

He passed the lot. Then somewhere near the cold-drink stand, without any help from anyone at all, he slowed to a stop.

Nine

The crowd lifted him onto their shoulders, they dipped the bike in bronze, and gave him three cheers.

By the time Bernice and everyone else arrived, Hugh had shaken hands at least twice with each person in the crowd, his photo had been taken eleven times and he'd signed an autograph book. He was famous.

'The Fast Bicycle Ride Down The Hill Cure,' Bernice said. 'I'd forgotten all about that one. I should have

known it would work.'

One-of-the-Best congratulated him, and even Rotten Frank admitted defeat. Somebody took a photo of them both for Frank to put on his wall at home and throw darts at.

The rest of the day went as smooth as old lino for Hugh. He climbed the steps to the winner's platform without tripping, he shook hands with the judge and remembered to let go, and he mingled with the guests of honour without standing on anyone's toes.

He couldn't do a thing wrong.

'He's cured!' his mum said.

'At last,' his dad agreed.

'I told you I'd fix you up,' Bernice said.

And to make the day a perfect success, Hugh was awarded a special prize. A set of six crystal glasses, with a matching jug.

He broke the jug on the way home in the car. But all the glasses made it back. Well, four of them did, anyway.

From Max Dann

The idea for *Bernice Knows Best* was inspired by true events. When I was young, I knew a girl who was definitely quite accident-prone. I am happy to report that she has long grown out of it, and is completely cured – well amost.

From Stephen Axelsen

It's great that Hugh is all fixed up finally. But is it really? I can't help wondering if Bernice will still find Hugh interesting now that her work is done. If I were him, I would pretend to be clumsy again from time to time. Or I'd ask her to teach me how to be a knife-juggling bungie-jumper, for instance.

On second thoughts, it might be safer if they become ordinary everyday normal friends, and just bake the occasional cake.